The Ribbit Exhibit

One frog's tale of a leap of faith

Always stick up for the "underfrogs"!
Nicole DeRosa Cannella

Nicole DeRosa Cannella
Illustrations by Brian Rice

AuthorHouse™
1663 Liberty Drive
Bloomington, IN 47403
www.authorhouse.com
Phone: 1-800-839-8640

First published by AuthorHouse 03/23/2013

ISBN: 978-1-4634-2435-0 (sc)
978-1-4817-3606-0 (e)

Library of Congress Control Number: 2011913113

Printed in the United States of America

To my loving family and friends who believed in and encouraged my endeavor all along. To God for giving me the means to write and to all of the 'underfrogs' who will see that you can rise above being bullied.

Billy the Bullfrog was a bully.
I never understood why.
Sometimes he would shove me
as he hopped on by.

I did not ask for any trouble-
kept mostly to myself,
but often he would pull my backpack
right off my cubby shelf.

One morning on the playground,
he and his friends made fun-
of me in my new rain boots
until recess was all done.

Then in the cafeteria
as we all sat down to eat,
he stole away my lunchbox-
and ate my chocolate treat.

I pretended it did not matter,
I tried to walk away-
but I was scared to go to school
each and every day.

I am not like the other frogs-
not loud, or funny or strong.
I am not sure who'll be my friend,
or with what group I belong.

This Thursday
Audition
for the School Play
Don't forget to buy your
Milk
TODAY!

One day, Miss Trombelina said
"Now children, eyes up here...
I want you all to write a tale
about what it is you fear."

"Now write this in your notebooks..."
She said and wrote with chalk.
"This assignment will share your worries
and what scares you as a frog."

"Now maybe some among you
are scared when in the dark,
fear fireflies or fishing nets
or tall slides at the park..."

"...Write with honest feeling
and draw a picture to illustrate-
your story and we'll hang it up
to see on Parent's Day."

"Do not be embarrassed
for everyone has fears-
nobody will laugh at you
for what you choose to share."

"We'll call the show the Ribbit Exhibit
And you'll be proud to say,
you told your tale with total truth
to share on Parent's Day."

THE RIBBIT EXHIBIT

That night as I got writing,
on my project for the week-
I feared that if I told my story
I'd be forever called a 'geek'.

But maybe if I told the truth
about the bullying of Billy Bullfrog
the teachers and kids would all speak up
and he'd be forced to stop.

And so, I got to writing,
I put it all on paper-
The teasing and the bullying...
how I wish that I felt safer.

I drew some pictures too
of days that I recall-
when I was squished into my cubby,
or tripped while in the hall.

I shared my tale with total truth,
I did not tell a lie.
And when I closed my notebook up,
I began to cry.

I felt afraid I'd make it worse-
And Billy would be more cruel.
I'd have to move so far away,
and join another school.

I brought in my assignment-
Despite my being scared.
Parent's Day had now arrived.
I tried to hide my fear.

Up there on the wall,
was a picture that I drew
of me alone at lunchtime-
like everyday at school.

My story was there beside it,
hung up with sticky tape.
I reached the point of no return...
I had to face my fate.

THE RIBBIT EXHIBIT

When the frogs stopped there to read it,
I saw tears in some wide eyes...
Even Billy's mother
wiped her green cheeks as she cried.

"I did not know you felt this way."
Said Miss Trombelina as she read.
She whispered my story to herself-
and bowed her froggy head.

I did not write Billy's name in it
I kept him from that shame.
For even though he hurt me so,
I did not want to do the same.

BBIT EXHIBIT
EXHIBIT

The most popular kids at school,
they even like my story...
They told me that they 'had my back'
and I never had to worry.

Fiona the fancy frog
hopped up to me to say,
that I could sit with her at lunch
each and every day.

I was feeling really good inside,
but then I realized...
that Billy was looking right at me
with his giant Bullfrog eyes.

60

As he hopped straight up to me,
I thought of hopping away-
but I held my ground and waited for
what it was he had to say...

"I know it was me you wrote about-
and I think it's really cool,
that you didn't write my name in it
to share with the whole school."

"...I guess I can be sort of rough,
and show off my big size-
but it is kind of wimpy
to pick on the different guy."

And as I hopped away from him,
I lifted up my head...
For tomorrow's day at school was one-
I didn't have to dread.

The End.

THE RIBBIT EXHIBIT

CPSIA information can be obtained
at www.ICGtesting.com
Printed in the USA
LVIC010059230413
330390LV00003B